THE BINDER OF
DOOM
BOA CONSTRUCTOR

by Troy Cummings

BRANCHES

SCHOLASTIC INC.

TABLE OF CONTENTS

To Penny. I love all the things you draw, sculpt, weave, and glue together. Thanks for the inspiration!

Copyright © 2019 by Troy Cummings

All rights reserved. Published by Scholastic Inc., *Publishers since 1920.* SCHOLASTIC, BRANCHES, and associated logos are trademarks and/or registered trademarks of Scholastic Inc.

The publisher does not have any control over and does not assume any responsibility for author or third-party websites or their content.

Library of Congress Cataloging-in-Publication Data

Names: Cummings, Troy, author.

Title: Boa constructor / by Troy Cummings.

Description: First edition. | New York, NY : Branches/Scholastic Inc., 2019. | Series: The binder of doom ; 2 |

Summary: Something is stealing machine parts from all over Stermont, including a wrecking ball from a local construction site, and Alexander and his fellow monster hunters, Rip, and Nikki, fear that it is building a Stermont-smashing machine – so the friends must use the resources of the summer maker program at the library to stop this monster, and perhaps even solve the mystery of who is leaving monster trading cards where the Super Secret Monster Patrol can find them.

Identifiers: LCCN 2018058516| ISBN 9781338314700 (hardcover) | ISBN 9781338314694 (pbk.)

Subjects: LCSH: Monsters – Juvenile fiction. | Construction equipment – Juvenile fiction. | Makerspaces in libraries – Juvenile fiction. | Public libraries – Juvenile fiction. | Best friends – Juvenile fiction. | Horror tales. | CYAC: Monsters--Fiction. | Construction equipment – Fiction. | Makerspaces – Fiction. | Libraries – Fiction. | Best friends – Fiction. | Friendship – Fiction. | Horror stories. | LCGFT: Horror fiction.

Classification: LCC PZ7.C91494 Bo 2019 | DDC 813.6 [Fic] – dc23 LC record available at https://lccn.loc.gov/2018058516

10 9 8 7 6 5 4 3 2 1   19 20 21 22 23

Printed in China   62

First edition, September 2019

Edited by Katie Carella

Book design by Troy Cummings and Sarah Dvojack

CHAPTER 1

THE HEADLESS DUCK

In the middle of the night, Alexander Bopp heard a strange clicking sound.

He sat up in bed.

CLICKETY-CLICK.

There it is again! he thought. He held his breath. Something was moving underneath his bed.

WHIRRR...CLICKETY-CLICK!

Alexander did what most kids would do in this situation: He ducked under his blanket.

But unlike most kids, Alexander wasn't hiding. He was setting a trap.

Alexander was the leader of the Super Secret Monster Patrol, a group of kids sworn to protect Stermont from monsters. Recently, a whole slew of monsters had been unleashed on the town. The S.S.M.P. was going to be busier than ever.

WHIRRRR...CLICKETY-CLICK!

Alexander waited for the thing-under-the-bed to come out.

"GOTCHA!" he shouted. He dove to the floor, slamming his blanket down over the clicky thing.

The thing shook. It clicked. And then it quacked.

Alexander blinked.

He yanked off the blanket. He'd captured a windup toy duck. It was waddling in circles.

"Captain Duck!" said Alexander. "Who wound you up?"

SCREEE! A flapping bat-like creature swooped down from Alexander's bookshelf. Its claws were long. And pointy. And headed straight for Alexander's face.

"Yikes!" Alexander shielded himself with the toy duck.

VRRRRT! The creature's claws spun like a drill, unscrewing the large, yellow windup key from Captain Duck's back.

PLOP! The duck fell apart. Alexander gasped.

The bat-creature flapped out the window and disappeared into the night.

Alexander closed his window, locked it, and climbed back into bed.

The last thing he saw before falling asleep was Captain Duck's head looking up at him from the floor.

CHAPTER 2

A CARD AND A NOTE

"**R**ise and shine, porcupine!" his dad sang the next morning. "You need to get to the library! Summer camp starts in twenty-five minutes."

Alexander buried his head under his pillow.

"Nice try," said his dad. "Hey! What happened to Captain Duck?!"

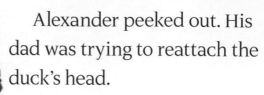

Alexander peeked out. His dad was trying to reattach the duck's head.

Alexander wanted to say, "A bat-monster flew in my window and stole the duck's windup key!" But he didn't say anything. Grown-ups didn't know about monsters — they couldn't see them.

"Well, come on. Let's have some breakfast," said his dad, heading downstairs.

Alexander rolled out of bed and got dressed. He paused. Something was sticking out of his sock drawer. A note? No. A folded-up monster trading card!

PEAR-O-DACTYL

Fruity flying dinosaur.

ATTACKS NOSEDIVE! **40** BLOSSOM-BOMB! **55**

HABITAT	DIET	TYPE

Jurassic fruit-baskets.

Goldfish. (Both kinds.)

FOOD

CRITTER

Pear-o-dactyls
love pointy hats.

Did a pear-o-dactyl break into my room last night? Alexander wondered. He reread the card. *No. Last night's monster wasn't wearing a hat.*

Alexander grabbed a binder off his desk. The word DOOM was written across the front. There were four other monster cards in there. Someone — or some*thing* — had been leaving them all over town. He added the pear-o-dactyl card to his collection.

"Al, hurry up!" his dad called. "Your eggs are ready! And I need to get to work to set up my new dental chair!"

Alexander tossed the binder in his backpack and headed downstairs.

He paused at the bottom step. A note peeked out from under the front door.

Alexander picked it up.

He smiled. Only two people called him Salamander: his best friends, Nikki and Rip. They were both members of the S.S.M.P. Secretly, they were also monsters — but they were *good* monsters.

NIKKI: A jampire. Loves eating red, juicy stuff, like raspberries.

Avoids sunlight.

Sees in the dark.

Has fangs.

RIP: Seems like an ordinary boy. But when he eats sweets, he transforms into a knuckle-fisted punch-smasher.

C-H-O-M-P!!!

Tail

Horns

Hairy fists

Rip keeps monster-ants in his pocket. When they eat sweets, they transform into gi-norm-ants.

Alexander read the note.

SALAMANDER!
I found the perfect spot for our new,
super-secret headquarters. It's totally
private, with a door that locks. It
even has its own bathroom!

DOWNTOWN

Meet us here
after breakfast.

-RIP

P.S. UGH. I had nothing to do with this.
It was all Rip's idea! -Nikki

P.P.S. That's true. I'm awesome! -RIP

P.P.P.S. Use the secret knock:
TAP. TAP. KICK-KICK-BAM!

Alexander wolfed down his scrambled eggs.

"Gotta run!" he told his dad. "I'm meeting Rip and Nikki before camp!"

"Have fun with your pals!" said his dad.

Alexander dashed out the door.

I can't wait to see our new S.S.M.P. headquarters! he thought.

A TIGHT SPOT

Alexander parked his bike near a construction site downtown.

Can this be the right place? he wondered.

Rip and Nikki were nowhere to be seen. But four letters had been stomped into the mud by size five boots:

"Rip tracks!" said Alexander.

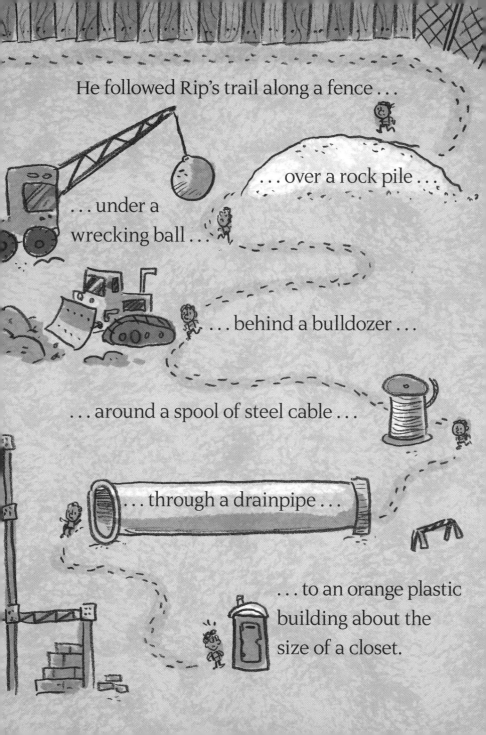

He followed Rip's trail along a fence . . .

. . . over a rock pile . . .

. . . under a
wrecking ball . . .

. . . behind a bulldozer . . .

. . . around a spool of steel cable . . .

. . . through a drainpipe . . .

. . . to an orange plastic
building about the
size of a closet.

THIS is our headquarters?! thought Alexander.

Alexander knocked. **TAP. TAP. KICK-KICK-BAM!**
The dial on the door slid from OCCUPIED to
AVAILABLE.

As the door swung open, Alexander was hit by two things:

1. The fake-fruity smell of bathroom cleaner.
2. The sound of Rip and Nikki arguing.

"Uh, hi," said Alexander, squeezing into the porta potty.

"Welcome to our new HQ!" said Rip.

"You mean *PU*!" said Nikki. "This place stinks!"

Their voices echoed. It sounded like their heads were in a bucket.

"Are you kidding?!" asked Rip. "This place is perfect!"

"Uh, it'll work for now," said Alexander, pinching his nose.

"Let's just get started," said Nikki. "Who has monster activities to report?"

"A bat-creature swooped into my room last night!" said Alexander. "Its claws spun like a drill, and it stole a windup key from my toy duck." He paused. "I also found *this*!"

He opened his binder.

"Another monster card?" said Nikki. "Who could —"

WHAM-WHAM-WHAM!

She was interrupted by angry pounding at the door.

THE BUILDERS

Alexander, Rip, and Nikki huddled together in the porta potty.

"Come outta there RIGHT NOW!" shouted an angry voice.

WHOOM! The door was yanked open.

A construction worker stared down at them. His eyebrows were low, and his mouth was a straight line, like a metal beam. He wore a tool belt, and coveralls that said MACK.

"You kids cannot be sneaking around my work site," growled Mack. "Especially not today! My wrecking ball's gone missing —and it's only 8 A.M.! So scram!"

The three friends sprinted away. Alexander pointed at the crane as they ran by. "The wrecking ball was there a few minutes ago," he said. "How could someone steal something so heavy?!"

"Beats me!" said Rip.

They ran all the way to the library.

"See you later, Rip!" said Nikki. "Salamander and I have to head inside now."

"Not so fast, weenies!" said Rip, grinning. "My mom signed me up for maker-camp, too! She said I was playing too many video games."

"Rip! That's great!" said Alexander.

They hurried inside.

Ms. Sprinkles, the librarian, was writing on the whiteboard.

"Ah! You three are just in time," she said, turning around. She smiled at Rip. "And you must be Rip. Welcome to the Stermont Summer Maker Program! Meet your fellow maker-bees: Becka, May, and Chuck."

Three kids waved to Rip from a worktable.

"Hiya, weenies!" said Rip.

Nikki elbowed him in the ribs. "OOF! I mean, hello, *maker-bees*," he added.

Becka, May, and Chuck gave Rip a funny look.

"This week, we're going to build machines," said Ms. Sprinkles.

"Cool!" everyone cheered.

"You each have to make a machine that performs a helpful task," said Ms. Sprinkles. "Here's our schedule for the week."

THIS WEEK'S MAKER-CHALLENGE

MONDAY:
Design your machine.

TUESDAY:
Build your machine.

WEDNESDAY:
Machine Share-Time!

PRIZES!

"Prizes?!" said Rip. "Sweet!"
The campers got right to work. Alexander spent the morning brainstorming.

By lunchtime, he had his idea:

Alexander spent the rest of the afternoon sketching his plans.

Before he knew it, it was time to leave.

"See you tomorrow, maker-bees!" said Ms. Sprinkles.

Alexander, Rip, and Nikki headed outside.

"Maker-camp rocks!" said Rip. "I'm totally going to win the maker-challenge!"

Alexander opened his mouth to reply, but then —

— a loud, long, bone-rattling buzzing noise blared across the town square.

WET CEMENT

The loud buzzing echoed in Alexander's ears.

"What was that?" he asked.

"An alarm?" Rip guessed. "I think it came from the work site."

"Let's check it out!" said Alexander.

"Just steer clear of Mack!" warned Nikki as they ran to the site.

They crouched behind a tool cart.

BZZZZZRT! Mack was pressing an ALERT button on his bullhorn.

"*That's* what we heard," whispered Nikki.

Alexander and Rip nodded.

The rest of the workers gathered around.

"Mack must be the boss," whispered Rip.

"Listen up, crew! First, someone stole our wrecking ball. Now, two more things have gone missing: the treads from our bulldozer and a spool of steel cable. I'm shutting down this work site until I find out what's going on here."

Alexander turned to whisper to his friends, but he bumped the cart.

CLANK! A hammer fell to the ground.

"HEY!" Mack shouted, rolling the cart aside. "I told you kids to scram!"

"Yessir!" said Rip. "We're scramming!"

The three friends scrammed. But as they reached the fence — **SPLOTCH-SPLOTCH-SPLOTCH!**

They'd run right across a patch of wet cement.

"Crud," said Alexander. "We're going to be in big trouble now!"

"I'll fix this!" said Rip. He grabbed a stick and added some marks to the cement.

"Uh, thanks, Rip," said Alexander, with an eye-roll. Then he knelt down for a closer look. "What's that thing?" He picked up something green and shiny from the cement and showed it to his friends.

"It looks like a guitar pick," said Nikki. She put the shiny green thing in her pocket.

As the three friends were leaving the work site, they came upon the porta potty — or what was left of it.

"Our headquarters is totally mangled!" Rip yelled.

The porta potty's sides were squeezed in. It looked like a giant soda can that had been crushed. And there were four holes punched through the roof.

"Yikes!" said Alexander. "Whatever squeezed that porta potty must have been huge!"

"We could've been in there . . ." said Nikki.

"Mack was right — this work site isn't safe." Alexander gulped. "Let's go home and just meet at the playground tomorrow morning."

PLAYGROUND PROBLEMS

The next morning, Alexander was out the door five seconds after breakfast.

"See ya, Dad!" said Alexander. He hopped on his bike and — **FLOMP!** He fell over.

"Careful, kiddo!" said his dad, running to the driveway.

Alexander checked out his bike. "My gears are gone!" he said. "I can't ride my bike without any pedals!"

"That's odd," said his dad. "The up-and-down lever on my dental chair disappeared yesterday, too. My patient got stuck up high!"

Alexander raised an eyebrow. *Two more stolen parts . . .* he thought.

"Since your bike is broken," said his dad, "you can ride *my* old set of wheels!"

Alexander's dad ran to the garage, and returned with a dusty skateboard and a helmet.

"Have fun skateboarding to camp!" he said.

"Uh, thanks," said Alexander, snapping on the helmet. He hugged his dad and skated down the sidewalk.

Unfortunately, Alexander didn't know how to skate.

He crashed eight times before he decided to run instead.

Alexander arrived at the park sweaty and out of breath.

"Ahoy, Salamander!" Nikki called down from the deck of a tugboat.

Alexander climbed aboard.

Rip slid down a pole to join them. "We can see downtown Stermont from up here!" he said. "This tugboat could be our headquarters!"

"But it's not secret at all," said Alexander.

"Yeah," Nikki agreed. "Anyone in the park could hear our battle plans."

They waited for a couple of toddlers to run by before they started their meeting.

"Look what I found this morning on my back deck," whispered Nikki.

"Another monster card!" said Rip.

INSIDE-OUT TROUT

LEVEL 10

It takes guts to battle this monster!

| ATTACKS | BLADDER-BATTER! | 40 | SPLEEN-SPLAT! | 80 |

HABITAT

Tackle boxes.

DIET

Bait smoothies.

TYPE

CRITTER

GROSS

On cold days, inside-out trouts wear reversible jackets.

Alexander tucked the card into his binder.

"There's definitely something fishy about these cards," said Rip. "And hey — what's with the skateboard? Where's your bike?"

"My bike gears were stolen," said Alexander. "And I think stuff is being stolen from machines all over town — not just from Mack's work site! A lever from my dad's dental chair went missing."

"Oh, that reminds me!" said Rip. "My mom said her wheelbarrow was missing its wheel this morning, too!"

Alexander made a list.

STOLEN MECHANICAL STUFF

* Captain Duck's windup key
* Wrecking ball
* Bulldozer treads
* Spool of steel cable
* Bike gears
* Dental chair lever
* Wheelbarrow wheel

"Why would someone take all those gears and levers and stuff?" asked Nikki.

"Maybe they're building some kind of machine," Alexander guessed.

"Speaking of machines, we should get to maker-camp!"

The friends ran to the library.

They spent the entire day on their projects.

Alexander worked through lunch on his monster alarm. He glanced over at Rip and Nikki, who were just as focused on their machines. Before he knew it, it was time to go.

"So, Rip, what are you making?" asked Alexander.

"It's top secret!" said Rip, shoving his machine into his bag. "You'll find out tomorrow."

They left the library and passed a screaming toddler as they entered the park.

"WAAAAAH!" The toddler threw his lollipop to the ground.

"That kid's having a meltdown!" said Alexander.

"I can see why," said Nikki. "Look!" She pointed to the playground.

Actually, she pointed to nothing. There was a muddy pit where the playground equipment used to be.

"We were here this morning! And now the entire playground is gone?!" said Alexander. "Where did it go?"

"It was stolen!" said Rip. "I bet the machine-swiping monster was here!"

"You could be right," said Nikki. "Swings and seesaws *are* like simple machines..."

Alexander nodded. But then —

SCREEE! A bat-creature swooped down, clamped its claws on Rip's bag, and lifted him into the air.

TOTALLY BATTY

"**G**et your claws off my bag!" Rip shouted to the bat-creature.

Alexander and Nikki grabbed Rip's legs.

"That's the bat-thing I saw in my room!" shouted Alexander.

"It looks like it's made from scrap metal!" said Nikki.

FLAPPA-FLAPPA-FLAP!

The bat-creature dragged the three friends toward the park entrance.

"Rip!" said Nikki. "Just let go of your bag!"

"No way!" said Rip. "My machine is in there!"

"*Of course!*" said Alexander. "It wants to steal your machine — just like it stole my windup key! This bat must be the machine-stealing monster!"

"Feed me something sweet!" Rip yelled. "I'll stop this junk pile with my monster powers!"

"I wish I'd brought a cookie or something," said Alexander.

Just then, a few ants crawled out of Rip's pocket and fell to the ground.

SCREE! The junk-bat flapped harder.

Alexander's heels lifted off the ground. Then he heard a noise from below.

BA-DINK! BA-DINK! Rip's ants had transformed into gi-norm-ants after chomping on the toddler's half-eaten lollipop.

That's it! thought Alexander. He let go of Rip and grabbed the lollipop.

"Nikki, catch!" he shouted as he tossed it to her.

She caught it, and lifted it up to Rip's mouth.

CHOMP! Rip bit into the lollipop.

RAWWRRRR!!! He transformed into MONSTER-RIP, the knuckle-fisted punch-smasher.

Monster-Rip sucker punched the junk-bat.

WHAM!

SCREEEEE! The mechanical monster flew off, releasing Rip's bag.

PLOOOF! Rip and Nikki landed in the sandbox.

Rip was stunned, but back to normal. "Ugh," he groaned. "Tug-of-war is less fun when *you're* the rope!"

Rip's ants marched over, carrying shiny green things on their backs.

"Look! My little buddies found more guitar picks!" said Rip.

Nikki took one from an ant and studied it for a moment. "I wonder where they're all coming from," she said as she put it in her pocket.

"Clearly a rock star trashed our headquarters," said Rip.

Alexander laughed. "Well, whether it was a rock star or a rock-star *monster*, we should head home," he said. "Lock your windows tonight in case the junk-bat returns!"

HIGH WIRE

The next morning, Alexander tried skating again. He made it all the way to his neighbor's yard before crashing into a bush.

"Hey, weenie!" Rip had skated over on his own board. "Since you wiped out a million times yesterday, I made you this!" he said. He handed Alexander a folded-up sheet of paper.

Do you like standing around AND moving really fast at the SAME TIME?

Do you like having skinned-up knees? (And elbows and palms and hips and chin?)

Do you like showing off how AWESOME you are?

Did you say YES?! Then you're ready for:

RIP'S GUIDE TO SKATEBOARDING!

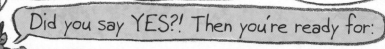

HISTORY

Skateboarding was invented seventy-five years ago when a surfer crashed into a roller-skater. Probably.

 My board! My wheels! BONK!!! Awesome!

Or 3,500 years ago when an Egyptian queen tripped over a stone tablet and some golden cups, and accidentally rode them down a pyramid.

Yeah! That sounds cooler. Forget the surfer thing!

HOW TO SKATE

1 STAND ON YOUR BOARD

2 GO FAST!!!!

3* DON'T FALL OFF. DUH.

*If you're having trouble with step 3, it means you're not doing enough tricks.

SEE NEXT PAGE.

RIP'S GR8 SK8 TRICKS!

NOTE: Real sk8ers use 8's instead of letters because it looks SO COOL! Try this practice sentence: My gr8 uncle N8's roomm8 K8 8 a pl8 of b8 on a dinner d8.

The easy-ski

The sea turtle

The balloon goon

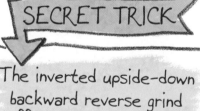

SECRET TRICK

The inverted upside-down backward reverse grind off a megalodon's tooth.

WARNING: You must be at least this awesome to attempt this trick.

When Alexander and Rip got to the town square, they saw Nikki looking up at the sky.

A shiny silver line stretched above downtown Stermont. It ran from the top of the work site, across the square, and into the woods behind the library.

"What is that thing?" asked Rip as they rushed over.

"It definitely wasn't there yesterday," said Alexander.

"Maybe it's a new power line?" Nikki guessed.

Alexander gasped. "Remember how Mack said a spool of steel cable was stolen? It must be that!"

"Let's worry about the cable later," said Rip. "I wanna get to maker-camp!"

Rip led Alexander and Nikki into the library. They plopped down near the stage.

"I have exciting news, maker-bees," said Ms. Sprinkles. "This morning, we're going to hear from a special guest. He's an expert at making things."

"Awesome!" Rip whispered to Alexander and Nikki.

"Please welcome the best builder in Stermont, Mr. Mackenzie Mackinaw!" said Ms. Sprinkles.

The campers clapped as a man in a hard hat took the stage. He carried a rolled-up blue poster.

Alexander, Rip, and Nikki stopped clapping. Mack the construction worker stood before them.

Mack smiled at all the kids. Until he noticed Alexander and his friends. Then he narrowed his eyes. "*You're* here?" he growled. He turned to Ms. Sprinkles. "Watch out for these three. They're snoopers!"

Ms. Sprinkles laughed. "They're curious children, for sure. But we all know curiosity leads to creativity!" She winked at Alexander.

Alexander smiled.

"So, Mr. Mackinaw," Ms. Sprinkles continued, "could you tell us about your latest project?"

"Uh, sure," said Mack. "My crew is building Stermont's new sports arena. We always start by drawing blueprints. Here, let me show you."

He unrolled his poster.

"Super cool!" said Becka.

"Yeah," Mack agreed. "At least, it *would* be super cool if we could finish the project. But things keep going wrong at the work site."

He shot Alexander another look.

"That's too bad, Mr. Mackinaw," said Ms. Sprinkles. "Do you have any advice for our young builders?"

"You bet," said Mack. "Always carry a screwdriver. And never play on wet cement!"

He glared at Alexander again. "Any questions?" asked Mack.

"Yes," said Alexander. "What's that steel cable for that's stretched across town?"

Mack peered out the window. Then he frowned.

"Uh, thanks for inviting me, Ms. Sprinkles — I have to go!" said Mack. He grabbed his blueprint and ran. As he jumped from the stage, Alexander saw something small, green, and shiny fall from his boot.

A HUNCH AT LUNCH

"**L**et's eat outside today," said Ms. Sprinkles, when lunchtime rolled around. "Then we'll have Machine Share-Time after lunch. Follow me, maker-bees!"

Alexander, Rip, and Nikki walked a few steps behind Becka, May, and Chuck.

"Look what fell off Mack's boot," whispered Alexander. "Another green thing!"

"So those guitar pick things are all his?" asked Rip.

"I actually don't think they're guitar picks," said Nikki. She pulled a few green things from her pocket. "They're too big. And they're kind of sharp."

Alexander was staring at the work site.

"Hang on," he said. "If the monster is building something . . . and *Mack* is the best builder in Stermont . . ."

Nikki's eyebrows shot up. ". . . then Mack could be a monster, too!" she said.

"Mack could be the junk-bat's boss!" added Rip.

They ate lunch on a bench near City Hall. Nearby, people were ordering food from a taco truck.

49

Alexander's eyes widened. "Mack's over there!"

"Let's get snooping!" said Rip.

They crept over. Mack was using his wrench to take bolts off the top of the truck.

The lady in the taco truck shouted up to Mack. "Thanks for your help! I can't believe someone stole my awning!"

"Stuff's getting swiped all over town," said Mack. "It's probably these pesky kids I keep running into."

"He's blaming *us* for the stolen stuff?!" Rip whispered.

"Classic monster move," Nikki whispered back.

"That should be a little better," Mack said, climbing down from the truck. "Now if you'll excuse me, I really need to see what's up with that cable stretched over the town square."

He ran to the work site.

"We should investigate that cable, too," said Alexander.

"For sure!" said Rip. "Just as soon as my machine wins the maker-challenge."

Alexander stood up. "We need to stop the Mack-monster, Rip. We should go now!"

"But the contest is about to start!" said Rip.

"Fine, but we'll leave right after share-time," said Nikki. "After we *finally* see your top secret project."

THE GREEN BLUEPRINT

After lunch, Ms. Sprinkles gathered everyone around the stage.

"Helloooooo, maker-bees!" she said, in a cheesy game-show voice. "Welcome to Machine Share-Time!"

One by one, the campers showed their machines.

Alexander:
Bedroom alarm

Keeps monst – I mean, burglars – from getting in your window!

"These are *all* such wonderful creations!" said Ms. Sprinkles.

She gave each camper an award.

Rip's shoulders slumped as he read his award.

"Oh, Rip," said Ms. Sprinkles. "These machines are supposed to help people. It's not helpful to smash things."

"Huh?!" said Rip. "Of course, it's helpful. Watch!"

Rip took a walnut from his bag and set it on the floor. Then he turned on his remote control.

CRUNCH! The bonker cracked the nut neatly in two.

Ms. Sprinkles laughed and changed Rip's award.

surprising!
MOST DANGEROUS MACHINE:
Bonker

Rip grinned, and gave his nutcracker a pat on the mallet.

The campers all exchanged high fives and fist bumps as they checked out one another's machines.

Alexander tapped Rip's shoulder. "Time to go," he whispered. "We've got a monster to catch!"

Rip drove his bonker to his cubby, tossed it in his bag, and gasped.

There was a monster card in his cubby.

DREARY-EAR

LEVEL **7**

It hears every secret you whisper!

| ATTACKS | WAX-THWACK! | 30 | LOBE-PROBE! | 70 |

HABITAT

Earmuffs.

DIET

Scary sounds.
(Creaky floorboards, howling wolves, and your uncle's snoring.)

TYPE

GROSS

?

UNKNOWN

 Dreary-ears can hear a ladybug scratch its chin.

"This is a weird one," said Alexander, tucking the card into his binder. "But we need to stay focused on Mack. Let's go!"

The friends raced into the work site.

The first floor was dark, and quiet.

"This place is creepy when no one's here," whispered Alexander.

Nikki peered around the dark room. "Mack must be here somewhere," she said. "I see his tool belt on that workbench over there."

"Unlike you, Salamander and I can't see in the dark," said Rip. "I'll turn on the lights." He felt along the wall and flipped a switch.

HUMMMMMMM!!

"What's that noise?" asked Alexander. He pulled a flashlight from his backpack and turned it on.

Mack's tool belt was floating in midair.

Rip's eyes grew wide. "Mack's tools are haunted!" he said.

Nikki laughed. "That wasn't a light switch, Rip! You turned on a giant magnet!" She pointed to an electric magnet hanging high above them.

Rip shrugged, and flipped the switch off. **CLANG!** The tool belt fell to the ground.

"Who's there?!" Mack called from the next room.

"He's coming this way! Let's move," whispered Alexander.

The three friends put on hard hats and climbed a nearby ladder. They tiptoed along the second-story beams like pirates walking planks. Finally, they stood directly above Mack's workbench.

Mack entered the room and turned on the lights. He walked over to the workbench.

"How did this get down here?" he said to himself. Mack reached for his tool belt.

Then he paused. He saw something beneath the workbench.

He reached under and pulled out a rolled-up poster. It looked like a blueprint, but it was printed on shiny green paper.

THE

S.M.O.O.S.H.E.R.

STERMONT **M**ASHING
OBNOXIOUSLY **O**VERSIZED
STEEL-**H**EADED
ENVIRONMENT-**R**UINER

CONTROL KEY
JUST WIND UP AND SMOOSH!

STOLEN LEVERS
STEAL SMART. STEAL LOCAL.

CONTROL PANEL

KID-CATCHER
LAUNCHES AWNING TO WRAP, TRAP, AND KIDNAP.

TUGBOAT
FULL STEAM.
A HEAD!

SWING-SET ARM
WHEEEEEE!!

WRECKING BALL
HEADS UP!

MONKEY BARS
ARM, AND DANGEROUS.

TWISTY SLIDE
SHAKE A LEG!

STEAM-SHOVEL SCOOP
CAN YOU DIG IT?

TINY WHEEL
SO CUTE!

STEEL BEAMS, CEMENT, NUTS, BOLTS, AND LUMBER
SWIPED FROM CONSTRUCTION SITE!

BULLDOZER TREADS
GOOD TRACTION!

DESTRUCTO-BATS
SEARCH FOR PARTS!

PATH OF THE S.M.O.O.S.H.E.R.

WOODS

DOWNTOWN STERMONT!

MACK ATTACK

Alexander squinted down at the green blueprint on Mack's workbench. "Look! That town-crushing machine has a wrecking ball!" he whispered. "And bulldozer treads!"

"And a wheelbarrow wheel!" added Rip.

"I see *tons* of stolen parts!" whispered Nikki.

Rip cupped his hands around his mouth, and shouted, "GIVE IT UP, MONSTER! WE'VE GOT YOU SURROUNDED!"

"Huh?!" said Mack, looking up.

Alexander, Rip, and Nikki jumped down onto the workbench.

"Ugh," said Mack. "You three again?"

SSSSSSS! There was a loud hissing sound from high above.

"We know you've been stealing parts to build your evil machine!" said Nikki, pointing at the S.M.O.O.S.H.E.R. plans.

"I don't know what you're talking about," said Mack.

"Why would I rob my own work site? And my blueprints are all blue — I have no idea where this one came from!"

Mack adjusted his hard hat. A shiny green thing fell off and fluttered to the ground.

"A-ha!" said Rip, picking it up.

"What the heck are those things?" said Mack. "I've been finding them everywhere."

"You're the one who's been dropping them! They're more proof you're a monster!" yelled Rip.

WHOOSH! A shadow moved overhead, but Mack didn't seem to notice.

Alexander swallowed. "Uh-oh . . ." he said. "I don't think Mack is a monster."

Mack sighed. "Look. You kids need to go play somewhere else. I just stopped by to grab my tool belt."

He looked around. Then he scowled.

"It's gone!" he said. He threw up his arms. "That does it! I'm tired of stuff getting swiped right under my nose. I'm heading home!"

Mack stomped out of the work site.

"I guess we were wrong about Mack," said Rip.

"Then who is building that Stermont-destroying machine?" asked Nikki.

SSSSSSS!! There was another loud hiss from above.

An enormous snake head peered down from the beams. It smiled, flicking its forked tongue between its fangs.

"Let usssss exssssssplain!" it said.

CHAPTER 12

LEFTY AND LUMPY

The snake-monster had a massive body with two heads and a wrench at the end of its tail. And it was wearing Mack's tool belt.

"Hello, sssquishy humansss," said the head on the right. "We're the boa consssstructor."

Lefty: The bossy head.

Lumpy: Does most of the work.

The snake's scales flashed green as it slowly slid down the steel beam.

"The green things we've been finding all over town — they're your scales!" said Nikki.

"Yesss, they fall off when we're angry," said the left head.

"Lefty and I have been gathering partsss for our massster project," said the right head.

"We would have finished yesssterday if Lumpy here hadn't lost the plans!" said Lefty.

"I didn't lose them — you did!" said Lumpy. The snake's tail coiled around the S.M.O.O.S.H.E.R. plans. "Anyhow, we have our drawing back. Let's build our machine so we can crush this town — just like we crushed that porta potty hideout!"

"Think again!" said Rip. "Nobody's squishing *our* town — especially not a slimy-old snake!"

"Sssnakesss aren't ssslimy!" Lumpy hissed, shedding a few scales.

"Lumpy, get to work!" said Lefty. "Our helperssss can handle the humansss."

Alexander looked around. "I don't see any helpers," he said.

Lefty shouted into the bullhorn. "A LITTLE HELP, PLEASSSE!"

Then the boa constructor slithered up the beams and out of sight.

SCREEEEEE!

"Uh-oh," said Rip. "Another junk-bat!"

"Not just one!" said Nikki.

Alexander, Rip, and Nikki scattered as three more mechanical bats dive-bombed the work site.

"Watch out for their claws!" Rip shouted. He threw a brick at a bat.

CLINK! He clipped its wing. The bat spun in the air and then swooped at Nikki.

Nikki swung a sledgehammer, knocking the bat into a brick wall.

KER-PLASH! It exploded in a shower of bolts.

"We got one!" said Rip.

"But what about the rest of them?" asked Alexander.

A squadron of bats circled the room. Sparks flew as their metal wings scraped against the bricks. The S.S.M.P. was outnumbered.

SCREAMS ON THE BEAMS

The bat-monsters closed in on the three friends. Rip jabbed at one with a shovel. **CLANG!**

"It's no use!" said Nikki. "Their armor's way too strong!"

Alexander snapped his fingers. "They're made of metal!" He turned to Rip and Nikki. "Make a run for the workbench!"

Rip and Nikki scooted backward toward the bench. The bats swooped after them, claws extended. Alexander sprinted to the magnet switch. He flipped it on.

HUMMMMMMM!!!

CLONK! The junk-bats were sucked into the powerful magnet. They broke into pieces.

"Good thinking, Salamander!" said Nikki.

SSSSSSS! An angry hiss echoed from above.

"The boa constructor is up there!" said Alexander. "We've got to stop it — I mean *them!*"

They raced up ladders, jumped over holes, and dodged rolling barrels as they made their way to the top level of the work site.

Alexander felt dizzy from the view. He could see the rooftops of every building on the square. The stolen cable stretched from the uppermost beams of the work site down to the woods beyond Stermont.

CLINK-CLANK-POP! The boa constructor's wrench-like tail removed the barrel from a cement mixer.

"You're too late," said Lefty. "Thisss barrel is the last part we need to conssstruct our smassshing machine. Now let's get out of here!"

The snake's tail held up a set of gears and a chain.

"My bike gears!" said Alexander.

SNAP! The tail attached the gear to the steel cable. Then the boa constructor flung itself off the building, clamping its jaws onto the spinning gears.

"Sssooo long, sssuckerssssss!" hissed Lefty as the monster sailed down the cable.

THE FLYING BUCKET

Alexander watched the boa constructor disappear into the woods behind the library.

"The monster's using this cable like a zip line!" said Alexander.

"Then let's get zipping!" said Rip.

"But how?" said Nikki. "We can't slide down with our hands."

Alexander looked around. There was a giant bucket nearby. Chains connected the sides of the bucket to a large hook.

"There's our ride!" said Alexander.

Rip tossed the
hook over the steel
cable. The three
friends climbed
into the bucket and
shoved off.

WHOOOM! They rocketed
over downtown Stermont.
Sparks shot out of the hook
as it rubbed against the cable.
Alexander's bones shook.

"Wooo-hooo!" shouted Rip.

"My braces are rattling!" cried Nikki.

"I wish we'd slow down!" yelled Alexander.

Alexander got his wish.

The zip-bucket dipped below the treetops,
and—**PLOMP!** The S.S.M.P. were dumped in the
middle of the woods.

Alexander's head was spinning as he stood up.

There, before them, stood a shining, towering,
frightening . . .

. . . pile of junk.

"Wait," said Rip. "I thought that cold-blooded reptile was building a machine. All I see is one big junkyard!"

The boa constructor slithered from the bottom of the pile.

"These partsss are jussst the beginning," said Lefty. "Now watch my creation take shape!"

"You mean *my* creation!" argued Lumpy. "You only drew the S.M.O.O.S.H.E.R., Lefty! *I'm* the one who has to build it!"

Scales flew as the two heads snapped at each other. Then the tail slapped them both in the face.

"Jussst get to work already!" said Lefty.

With lightning speed, the boa constructor whirled around the mountain of junk, connecting parts with its wrench-like tail. In no time, the monster had assembled the junk into a three-story machine.

Alexander's jaw dropped. "The S.M.O.O.S.H.E.R. looks just like it did in the blueprint!" he said.

The boa constructor slithered to the top of the machine. It pulled a lever on the control panel.

"What's that lever do?" asked Rip.

Alexander thought about the green blueprint. "Rip! Nikki! DUCK!" he shouted. But he was too late.

KID-CATCHER
LAUNCHES AWNING TO WRAP, TRAP, AND KIDNAP.

FWIP! The taco awning shot out of the S.M.O.O.S.H.E.R.'s belly. It flew onto the three friends, wrapping them tightly.

HISSSSS-SSS-SSS-SSS! The boa constructor's heads laughed, making a sound like a leaky air mattress.

"Now activate the machine, Lumpy!" ordered Lefty.

Lumpy held up Captain Duck's windup key, and clicked it into place on the control panel. 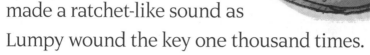 **CLACK-CLACK-CLACK-CLACK-CLACK-CLACK!** It made a ratchet-like sound as Lumpy wound the key one thousand times.

"The S.M.O.O.S.H.E.R. is like a giant windup toy!" said Alexander. "It won't stop as long as that key is spinning!"

"And we're trapped in here like a three-bean burrito!" said Rip.

Alexander, Rip, and Nikki hugged one another even tighter as the S.M.O.O.S.H.E.R. took a step toward downtown Stermont.

THE S.M.O.O.S.H.E.R.

WHAM! CRASH! BOOM!

With each step, the S.M.O.O.S.H.E.R. cleared a wide path through the forest.

"Those poor trees!" said Nikki.

"We can't let the S.M.O.O.S.H.E.R. get to town!" said Alexander.

"But what can we do?" said Rip.

"We can follow Mack's advice!" said Nikki, wriggling against the awning.

VVVVVRIP! She tore through the awning with a small silver tool.

"Always carry a screwdriver," she said.

Alexander, Rip, and Nikki burst free from the awning.

BOOM! The S.M.O.O.S.H.E.R.'s wrecking-ball arm knocked down a tree.

"Come on! Let's stop that giant hunk of junk!" said Alexander. "We just need to get ahold of that windup key!"

"Getting up to the control panel will be no problem," said Rip. "I've been climbing jungle gyms since I was two!"

Alexander, Rip, and Nikki ran toward the S.M.O.O.S.H.E.R. For each giant step it took, they took twenty kid-sized steps.

79

Finally, they hopped onto its foot. From there, they quickly climbed, swung, crawled, and bounced their way to the top.

"Stay out of sight," whispered Rip.

"Let'sss crusssh the library first!" yelled Lefty.

"No — the bank!" shouted Lumpy.

The boa constructor's heads were arguing about which building to destroy when they got to town.

"I see the key," whispered Alexander. He took a step toward the control panel.

"Not ssso fassst!"

FWISH! The boa constructor's tail whipped around Alexander, Rip, and Nikki.

Then it began to squeeze.

CHAPTER 16

SIMPLY SMASHING

"**O**OF!" Alexander felt the wind rush from his lungs as the boa constructor twisted around him and his friends.

BOOM! The S.M.O.O.S.H.E.R. took another earth-shaking step toward downtown Stermont. Alexander could see the library ahead of them.

"Sssweet!" hissed Lefty. "I'm going to dessstroy Ssstermont!"

"No!" snapped Lumpy. "*I'm* going to dessstroy Ssstermont! I did all the work!"

As the heads argued, the coil around the friends loosened. Alexander wriggled a leg free and kicked at the control panel. **VRRRT-CLONK!** His foot hit a lever.

WHOOSH! The wrecking ball swung out. **CLANG!** It smashed into Lumpy's head.

"OW!" cried Lumpy.

A shudder ran down the snake's body. Its coils loosened a bit more. Rip wiggled an arm free.

BOOM! The S.M.O.O.S.H.E.R. took another step toward the library.

"We can't let this machine . . .
destroy . . . Stermont!" gasped
Nikki.

Machine . . . destroy? thought
Alexander. He gasped. "That's it! Rip!
Use your bonker to get the key!"

Rip squirmed against the snake's
heavy coils. He freed the bonker
from his bag and turned it on with
his nose.

As the S.M.O.O.S.H.E.R. tromped through the
trees, Rip's bonker raced along the snake's coils,
swinging its mallet.

Lefty and Lumpy gulped.

"That's the tiny-but-powerful machine our helper tried to sssteal!" said Lefty. "Don't let it reach the key!"

Rip carefully steered the bonker with his teeth.

The boa constructor uncoiled itself.

Lefty and Lumpy lunged for the bonker, which had rolled off their coils and onto the S.M.O.O.S.H.E.R.'s control panel. But they were too late.

BONK!!

Rip's machine knocked the key out of its socket. **WHAM-WHAM-KER-PLAM!** The bonker pounded the key into a bent-up piece of scrap.

CLUNK-CLUNK-CLUNK-BRRRRUGHHH. The S.M.O.O.S.H.E.R. shuddered to a halt, tottered for a moment, and — **CRASH!**

It landed hard on its backside.

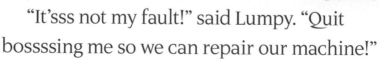

The two monster heads hissed at each other, baring their fangs.

"Thisss isss all your fault!" screamed Lefty.

"It'sss not my fault!" said Lumpy. "Quit bosssssing me so we can repair our machine!"

Rip's eyebrows rose as the two heads bickered. "Hey, Lumpy!" he shouted. "Lefty really thinks you screwed up!" He gave Nikki a wink.

Nikki caught on. "Hey, Lefty! Maybe Lumpy should be in charge!"

Lefty hissed at Lumpy. "You're too weak to be the bosssss!"

"Wanna bet?!" growled Lumpy.

"I'm going to sssink my fangs into you, Lumpy!" cried Lefty.

"I'll tear you to pieces!" roared Lumpy.

The two angry snake heads tied themselves into a clanking, hissing, snapping knot. And then —

KER-BLAMMMO!

The boa constructor wrenched itself apart.

Nuts, bolts, and metallic scales rained down, pattering against Alexander's, Rip's, and Nikki's hard hats.

The three friends high-fived and hopped off the S.M.O.O.S.H.E.R.

They walked through the woods to the edge of town, and sat on a stump.

"I'm so glad we kept Stermont from getting smooshed," said Alexander. He spotted a bit of paper wedged into one of the stump's roots. Another monster card!

BOA CONSTRUCTOR

LEVEL 2

Sneaky snake who likes to build — and DESTROY!

ATTACKS	DOUBLE-SNAP!	10	SIX-TON SQUEEZE!	20

HABITAT	DIET	TYPE
 Work sites, junk piles.	 Nuts. (Both kinds.)	THINGY CRITTER

The boa constructor's tail is smarter than its heads.

"Rats," said Alexander. "We're nowhere closer to knowing who left us these crazy cards."

"And we're nowhere closer to finding a new S.S.M.P. headquarters," grumbled Rip.

Nikki and Alexander smiled at each other.

"What's so funny?" said Rip.

THUMP-THUMP-THUMP. Nikki knocked on Rip's hard hat. "We've found our new headquarters — thanks to you and your bonker!" she said.

Alexander and Nikki turned Rip around.

Staring back at them was a three-story fortress made from broken machines, construction equipment, and playground parts.

"It's perfect!" said Rip.

"And it's super secret," said Nikki.

"And it's ours," said Alexander. He smiled at his friends. "Let's get to work!"

ABOUT THE AUTHOR

NEW YORK TIMES BESTSELLING AUTHOR
TROY CUMMINGS
Actually thinks two-headed snakes are kind of cool!

LEVEL **0**

| ATTACKS | EXTRA CONSSSONANTSSS | 77 | BENT WRENCH | 5 |

HABITAT
The art room in his house. (Assuming his kids let him use their markers.)

DIET
Three-bean burritos. Or, three bean burritos! He's not picky.

© H.S. INDUSTRIES

Troy Cummings has no tail, no wings, no fangs, no claws, and only one head. As a kid, he believed that monsters might really exist. Today, he's sure of it.

The idea for the BOA CONSTRUCTOR snuck up on Mr. Cummings while he was visiting a maker space in an elementary school library. (All the best ideas come from libraries!)

THE NOTEBOOK OF DOOM

SUBJECT: RISE OF THE BALLOON GOONS

Troy Cummings

Mr. Cummings has written and/or illustrated more than thirty books, including THE NOTEBOOK OF DOOM series.

THE BINDER OF DOOM
BOA CONSTRUCTOR
QUESTIONS & ACTIVITIES

Name three mechanical parts that go missing in the story. Can you spot them in the art on page 60?

Why does the S.S.M.P. think Mack is a monster? Find two clues!

A boa **constrictor** is a snake that squeezes its prey. Compare and contrast a boa constrictor to the boa **constructor**! List three similarities and three differences.

Rip suggests two locations for the new S.S.M.P. headquarters: a porta potty and a playground tugboat. Which of these makes a better headquarters? Explain, and use examples from the text to support your opinion.

Ms. Sprinkles asks the campers to invent a helpful machine. What machine would **you** invent? Draw and label a blueprint of your machine!